For
Alex and Karen
and also for Betty

First published 2013 by Walker Books Ltd
87 Vauxhall Walk, London SE11 5HJ
This edition published 2014
1 2 3 4 5 6 7 8 9 10
© 2013 Fiona Ross

The right of Fiona Ross to be identified as
author/illustrator of this work has been
asserted by her in accordance with the
Copyright, Designs and Patents Act 1988

This book has been typeset in Bodedo

Printed in China

British Library Cataloguing in Publication
Data: a catalogue record for this book is
available from the British Library

ISBN 978-1-4063-5453-9

WALKER BOOKS
AND SUBSIDIARIES

LONDON · BOSTON · SYDNEY · AUCKLAND

Down
the
alley,
a
gang
of
friends
partied.

They were the **Crazy Cat Crew.** They **loved** to **dance!**

Every night the Crazy Cat Crew whooped it up.
Sid moved, Griff grooved,
Budgie bopped, Nelson hopped.

And Arthur got down to the sounds from the streets. They revelled in the booming noise ... and it drove them CCCRAAZEEE!

However much they partied, one cat always slunk off first.

Oi, Arthur, having an early night?

But Arthur wasn't going to bed...

He loved wandering the streets scouring the bins for odds and ends, and rummaging for treasure.

One night a bright sparkle caught his eye.

It was a musical box and a pair of ballet shoes.

He excitedly opened the box and found a ballerina dancing to a lullaby.

Arthur put on the shoes and started to dance.

He hurried back to the alley to show his friends his latest treasure.

Ta dah!

The cats didn't like what they saw.

Sid poked fun at Arthur's new shoes.

HA HA HA!

The cats jeered and sneered but Arthur **didn't care.**

He was just **loving dancing!**

Nelson called an **urgent** meeting.

That's when Arthur knew he couldn't be part of the gang any more.

He packed his bags and left the alley.

The cats noticed that Arthur had gone.

Where are his things?

The Crazy Cat Crew romped, stomped and had a blast!

So the gang decided to look for Arthur and put things right.

And
when
they
finally
found
him,
they
asked
him
to
come
home.

Arthur was pleased as punch to be back down the alley with his friends.

every **Saturday night.**

Fiona Ross studied illustration and design for film and television. As a child she originally wanted to be an ice-cream-van driver, then a gymnast – and finally an illustrator. "It's a wonderful process," she says, "watching a story emerge and develop." Fiona lives and works in north London.

Also by Fiona Ross:

978-1-4063-3855-3

able from all good booksellers

www.walker.co.uk